Rainbow Rangers™

Meet the Team

[Imprint]
MAKE YOUR MARK
NEW YORK

IMPRINT

A part of Macmillan Publishing Group, LLC

120 Broadway, New York, NY 10271

Library of Congress Cataloging-in-Publication Data is available.

ISBN 978-1-250-19031-4 (trade paperback)

Our books may be purchased in bulk for promotional, educational, or business use. Please contact your local bookseller or the Macmillan Corporate and Premium Sales Department at (800) 221-7945 ext. 5442 or by email at MacmillanSpecialMarkets@macmillan.com.

Book design by Elynn Cohen
Imprint logo designed by Amanda Spielman

First edition, 2019

1 3 5 7 9 10 8 6 4 2

mackids.com

This book has a price,
You know that paying it is right,
Or else dragonflice
Will come to give you a fright.

THE RAINBOW RANGERS

are nature's superheroes.
They live in Kaleidoscopia.
It's a magical land on the
other side of the rainbow.

In this magical land,
there are beautiful animals.
Fluttercups fly after one another.

Dragonflice are always looking to play.

When the Rangers have a mission,
they go to the Crystal Command Center.
There is a Mirror of Marvels.

It shows them what happens on Earth.
When there is trouble,
the Rangers go to the rescue!

Three Rangers go on each mission.
They hop onto their Spectra-Scooters
and ride to the rescue.

Kalia chooses the Rangers for missions.
She is kind and smart.
Kalia loves and cares for the Rangers.
She helps them protect the Earth.

Rosie Redd leads the Rangers.
Her power is Super Strength.
She is very strong.

Rosie always knows what to do.
She never forgets to work as a team.

Mandarin Orange is always happy.
Her power is Super Hearing.
She can hear trouble from miles away.

Mandy sees the good in everyone.
She loves music
and has a song in her heart.

Bonnie Blueberry's power is Super Vision.
She can see very small things and
things that are very far away.

Bonnie invents cool machines.
Her Construct-O-Max tool
can make more machines by itself!

Indigo Allfruit has Super Speed.
With her Super Sonic Rainbow Sneakers
she can even run up walls!

Indy tells jokes and plays pranks.
She loves her friends.
She will do anything to make them smile.

Anna Banana is very sweet.
She can talk to any animal
and understand what it says.
Her power makes her the
Animal Whisperer.

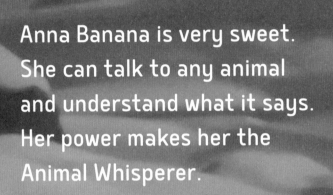

Anna is the heart of the team.
She loves everyone.
She loves cute animals most of all.

Pepper Mintz has Camouflage power.
That means she can blend in.
When she uses her Shimmer Shawl,
you cannot see her!

Pepper loves to read books.
She knows lots of facts
that help on missions.

Lavender LaViolette is hard to miss.
Her power is Flight. She has a Flitter Flower.
It makes her small and gives her wings.

Lavender loves to dress up.
She adores flowers and pretty things.

Floof is a Prismacorn.

He has rainbow hair and a magic horn.

He lives with the Rangers.

He goes with them on missions.

Floof can get into trouble.
He means well and he loves the Rangers.
The Rangers love him, too.

The Rangers are all different.
Sometimes, they do not agree.

They always know they are friends
and they are here to save the Earth,
so they always work it out.

The Rangers have saved the day many times.
They saved a baby polar bear
and took him back to his mom.

The Rangers have saved
a whale, an otter, a panda, and a bee.
They help forests, oceans, and cities.

The Earth needs someone to take care of it.
That is why Kalia is always watching.

And when she sees a problem,
she sends the Rangers.
They come from the other
side of the rainbow!

Ride, Rangers ride!